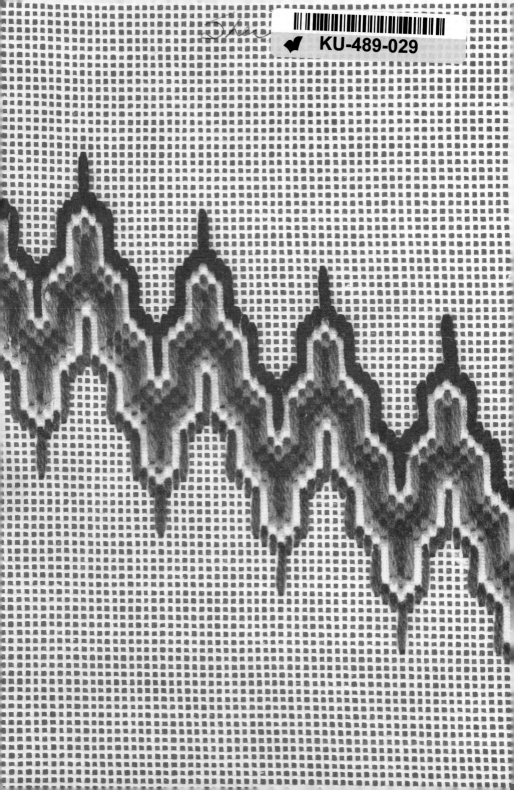

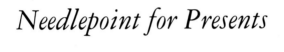

Needlepoint for Presents

Needlepoint for Presents

Anna Pearson

Webb&Bower
EXETER, ENGLAND

First published in Great Britain 1986 by
Webb & Bower (Publishers) Limited
9 Colleton Crescent, Exeter, Devon EX2 4BY

Copyright © text Anna Pearson 1986
Copyright © illustrations E.T. Archive Ltd 1986

Edited, designed and illustrated by
E.T. Archive Ltd, 9 Chelsea Wharf, 15 Lots Road
London SW10 0QH

Designed by Julian Holland
Photography by Eileen Tweedy
Drawings and charts by Cedric Robson
Production by Nick Facer

British Library Cataloguing in Publication Data
Pearson, Anna
    Needlepoint for presents. — (Crafts for presents; 2)
    1. Canvas embroidery
    I. Title   II. Series
    746.44'2   TT778.C3

ISBN 0-86350-091-9

Phototypeset by Tradespools Ltd, Frome, Somerset

Printed and bound in Hong Kong
by Mandarin Offset Marketing (HK) Ltd.

Contents

Introduction

Giving is as nice as receiving. This could not be better demonstrated than with a gift, planned and made with love, to say 'Thanks', to commemorate a birthday or anniversary, or just to show you are thinking of someone.

Of all crafts, needlepoint has probably enjoyed the greatest renewed interest—rightly so, for it is hard-wearing, practical, and suitable fibres in myriad colours are increasingly available.

The aim of this book is to show the enormous range of attractive items which are fun to stitch, very generous to give and extremely acceptable to receive. There are full working instructions for 27 items, which range from a tie tag which can easily and speedily be made, at a fraction of the cost of even a simple bunch of flowers, to suggestions for a once-in-a-lifetime present of dining chair seats worked perhaps by a group for a dear friend.

Materials and quantities are suggested in such a way that alternate colours can easily be substituted. The designs shown can be enlarged or reduced and I have proposed other applications that would make beautiful gifts.

Background

Needlework has always been closely related to the style of furniture that was current and fashionable, the fabrics which were within a family's means and the leisure time available to women for stitching decorative or purely utilitarian items.

The earliest surviving English needlepoint examples are cushions and table carpets dating from the sixteenth century, stitched by the ladies of great houses to make the plain wooden benches and simple tables more comfortable and attractive. Presents were stitched even then—Princess Elizabeth (later Queen Elizabeth I) wrote a prayer book and worked a needlepoint cover for it which she gave to her stepmother, Queen Catherine Parr.

Mary, Queen of Scots, imprisoned for seventeen years in the Earl of Shrewsbury's house, produced many wonderful pieces of needlework when working with Elizabeth, Countess of Shrewsbury.

In the early seventeenth century the family bed was often in the main reception room so it was considered extremely important to have beautiful bedhangings, and they were often the most valuable items in the house. They were frequently worked in needlepoint, especially flamepoint Florentine patterns. Later on, when velvet fabrics were introduced from Italy, needlepoint 'slips' were stitched and applied to the velvet ground fabric. 'Slips' are small—quick to work—floral or animal motifs worked on canvas, cut out and stitched to the softer, more pliable velvet.

As walnut and then mahogany was used in furniture making, the need to hide it disappeared and the table-carpet became a floor carpet. Wing and other upholstered chairs became popular, and floral designs in tent stitch and Florentine patterns were worked as tight upholstery.

When Adam introduced his carved and painted furniture in the eighteenth century, silk was considered a more suitable covering for these delicate pieces; so pictures, firescreens and purses are the needlework items which survive from this period.

In America, as in Britain and Europe, the needlewoman's surroundings dictated the type of stitching undertaken. The early settlers were far too busy building homes, and sometimes defending them, to indulge in fancy needlework. Clothes and household linens had to be sewn and frequently the women had to weave their own fabrics. Sewing of the early period was therefore largely utilitarian.

On the East Coast, especially in the settlements set up around the sea-ports, ladies were able to order embroidery supplies from sea captains sailing between England and the New World with furniture, fine fabrics and other special supplies. Fairly soon, needlepoint shops and schools were established to teach 'young ladies the ways of the needle'.

By Victorian times, there was a newly rich and leisured class in England, sadly often without taste. Berlin woolwork became the rage throughout Europe and America. Originally this work was stitched on canvas in soft colours following a hand-painted chart. As the demand grew, however, the colours became more garish and the patterns banal. Threads such as chenille (a thick furry thread) and beads were used; Turkey or Plush stitch was worked and then clipped to give a sculptural relief to flowers and birds.

The seaside holiday became popular, made fashionable by the Prince Regent with his building the Brighton Pavilion, and made accessible to everyone with the coming of the train. The resorts produced many little souvenir gifts and it is evident from the large number of needlework items such as pinholders, needlecases and thimbles just how popular needlepoint and needlework of all kinds became.

Today all types of canvas work, using Florentine, pictorial and geometric designs, are being enjoyed by an ever-increasing number of people who find stitching relaxing as well as stimulating.

Basic supplies and materials

Each project clearly lists the required materials and order of work. All designs are charted, and decorative stitches are explained in the Stitch index on page 54.

The types of materials available, together with tips for handling the different fibres, are briefly explained here.

Canvas
Regular mono or *single thread Zweigart canvas* has been used for all projects calling for mono canvas; the mesh is specified under each project. Follow it, otherwise the finished size will differ and the threads may not cover the canvas. White canvas rather than ecru has been used throughout. While this is a personal choice, it is obviously important to have white canvas where areas are left exposed (e.g., the Initial cushion and the herb sachets). The exact size needed is given but most shops will only sell canvas by the quarter or half metre; label any left over with the mesh and store for next time. Always bind the cut edges with masking tape (3.5 cm [1½ in] is good), or turn and stitch them.

Interlock mono canvas is also available; the threads are bonded together at each intersection rather than weaving over and under each other as with *regular canvas*. This *interlock canvas* is excellent for items where very close trimming is necessary but never use it for cushions or upholstered pieces where some 'give' is needed.

Plastic canvas is available in sheets about 26.5 × 34.5 cm (10½ × 13½ in) in both 7 and 10 mesh. It also comes in circles, hexagons and diamonds. No seam allowances are needed as the pieces are cut exactly to the thread count given in the instructions. It is important to cut pieces from the panel in the same direction and to trim all small nubs on the cut edges. Each of the projects is worked piece by piece, leaving one thread on each side unworked (this is shown on the charts); this thread is used for joining the pieces to make the finished box, basket, or other gift.

Perforated paper comes in white or ecru in sheets 23 × 30 cm (9 × 12 in) and it is easier to work the designs on a complete sheet, mounted on a small frame, before cutting out the individual panels.

Frames

Frames make one's work better in all cases except when using plastic canvas. Stitch tension is smoother, the canvas is easier to see and there is no distortion; it is impossible to work pulled thread stitches or use ribbons without one.

The most practical frame is assembled from artist stretcher bars; these are bought in pairs of varying lengths: for example, one pair of 30 cm (12 in) and one pair of 40 cm (16 in) would give a rectangular frame 30 × 40 cm (12 × 16 in). They can be reused with other lengths to make other dimensions. Fix the canvas on the assembled frame as tautly as possible, using drawing pins.

Threads

Appleton's Crewel wool has been used for all the projects stitched in wool and the relevant reference numbers are given. This wool comes in two quantities, a 25 gram hank, which has been used for the projects in the book, or a very small skein, which is useful if only a few stitches of a shade are needed. Always cut new hanks into two equal lengths to get a good working length and follow the strand count given with each stitch. This will vary depending on the size of stitch and mesh of canvas; the right number of strands will give good coverage and hard wear.

Stranded cotton
DMC cottons have been used. Check the manufacturer and reference number when buying, or substitute a similar colour from the range available—they are all the same thickness (6 strands) and length 8 m (9 yd). The cotton needs 'stripping' before use; cut a length about 50 cm (20 in) and pull the 6 individual strands apart. Lay them flat, side by side, and then thread the needle; this makes the cotton lie smoothly on the canvas and gives better coverage. Follow the instructions for the number of strands for a particular stitch.
Pearl cotton
This is used as it is. To prepare a new skein for use, take off the two wrappers, untwist the skein and cut through it twice, once at the knot holding it together and once at the opposite end; this will give two lots of threads approximately 48 cm (19 in) long. Thread the wrapper with the colour-way number back on one length and keep for reference.
Metallics
The easiest to use is *Balger 16* which comes in 10 metre skeins in gold, silver and other colours. *Twilley's Goldfingering* is also widely available. Cut the working lengths no longer than 40 cm (16 in) to avoid it unravelling.

Scissors

A small embroidery pair, a large pair for cutting canvas and a stitch-ripper for carefully ripping mistakes from the back of the canvas are useful.

Ribbons

All the ribbons used in the book are *Offray's double-faced satin* ribbons in either 1.5 mm ($\frac{1}{20}$ in) or 3 mm ($\frac{1}{10}$ in) width. Generally the narrower ribbon is used for stitching and the wider one couched or laid down and stitched in place with another thread. A normal tapestry needle is used but it is more satisfactory to work stitches in ribbon before working the adjoining areas.

Needles

Always use *Tapestry* needles; size 18 for plastic canvas, size 20 for 14 mesh and size 22 for 18 mesh.

Starting and finishing a new thread

To start, knot the thread at one end and sew in from the front of the canvas, leaving knot on surface near starting point of and in direction of work. (With ribbon it is not necessary to put a knot at the end, simply leave a tail.) When sewing reaches the knot or tail cut it off close to the canvas. The back of the stitches will have caught the thread firmly. To finish thread, run through the back of several stitches.

Design charts and Stitch index

Each project has a design chart showing the position of the stitches. All decorative stitches are also included in a 'Stitch index' on pages 54/59.

Marking the canvas

If the canvas needs to be marked, use either a pencil or a waterproof pen or tacking thread only.

If a pencil is used, give the marked canvas a good rub over with kitchen paper before starting work, as the 'lead' (graphite) is apt to make wool dirty.

Test any waterproof marker before use on the selvage of the canvas to make sure it is fast.

A tacking thread is the only possible method if areas of the canvas are to be left exposed and unstitched.

Presents for the home

During my twelve years teaching needle-point, I have found that cushions are by far the most popular thing my students, and people who buy my ready-to-go designs, want to work. They are not too ambitious, the final size is not crucial (as it might be if required to fit an upholstered piece, such as a chair or firescreen) and they are not difficult to make up although I always recommended professional making-up for any needlepoint. For example, the trellis panel has been mounted on the equivalent of a ready-made cushion bought complete with pad and zipped cover; it is simple to remove the cover, slip stitch the completed needlepoint panel centrally on the front, and zip back in place.

The tassels on the Initial cushion are quick to make and give a touch of lux-ury—they are made from leftover wool when the piece was finished.

The fine lace edging on the ribbon-lattice herb sachet was purchased ready-made but again adds a finishing touch that makes a pretty design into a beautiful present.

None of the designs is large—which in many ways makes them more acceptable: either of the cushions would look lovely on a small armchair or they would look good mixed in with existing cushions on a sofa. The Initial cushion (with the letter of your choice) would look beautiful on a bed. It is a simple matter to enlarge any of the designs; all that is needed is more canvas and thread. Along with specific details for these pieces are further ideas for additional uses for the designs.

Initial cushion

This is worked in crewel wool and pearl cotton with a Florentine border and a *Lace Cross stitch* background.

The initial is taken from the alphabet on pages 62/63 and is a good example of how to create a bold letter from a graph that is originally only 17 threads high. Instead of making each square on the graph represent 1 *Tent stitch* over 1 thread of canvas, each square represents 1 *Cushion stitch* over 2 threads of canvas—this automatically doubles the height and width of the letter.

A wonderful gift idea for this design was suggested to me by a friend whose daughter was about to get married. She made each of the bridesmaids a small cushion with their own initial in the honey shades of the dresses they wore on the big day. Another, if rather ambitious, idea is a double wedding kneeler which was made up and used for the marriage service and afterwards the needlepoint was upholstered on to a fender stool for the new home.

The border would also make a good-looking photograph frame either exactly as it is graphed here, to take a square print, or shortened by two or three patterns along the sides, to take an upright print.

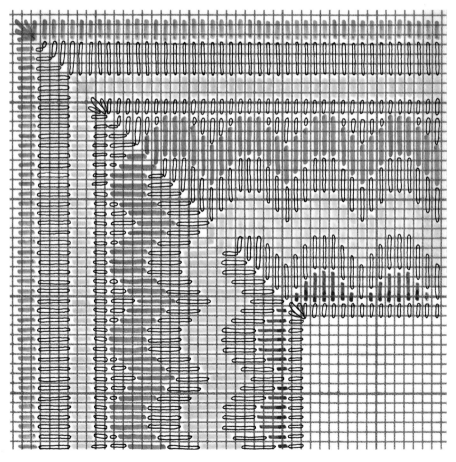

Materials

32 × 32 cm (13 × 13 in) 14 mesh white mono canvas. Finished size is 27 cm (11 in) square.
Crewel wool:
¼ hank Flamingo 1
½ hank Flamingo 2
½ hank Flamingo 3
DMC pearl cotton no 5: 2 balls or 4 skeins Ecru

Stitches to refer to in Stitch index:
Straight Gobelin over 2 threads
Straight Gobelin over 4 threads
Cushion
Lace Cross

Alphabet on pages 62/63

Find centre of canvas by folding. Count out 34 threads in all directions and mark with tacking thread. (This will give a central square of 68 × 68 threads for the initial.)

Starting with the innermost line of *Straight Gobelin*, work the border; use 4 strands crewel wool and a double strand of pearl cotton.

Work the initial in centre in *Cushion* using 3 strands crewel. Work background with 1 strand pearl cotton in *Lace Cross*.

Trellis design Florentine cushion

Florentine patterns are very popular as needlepoint designs; they grow quickly, they are not difficult (once a small area of pattern is on the canvas they are easy to work while watching television) and they can look totally different (modern or traditional) by the use of colour.

Trellis is a very adaptable design and surprisingly easy. In this soft colour scheme with a border it makes a pretty cushion; in darker colours and without the border it is an excellent choice for upholstery (see the dining chair suggestions) and worked on 18 mesh canvas in stranded cottons, it looks beautiful as an evening bag front (page 27).

Work the trellis first and then the border. For a larger cushion, just work more of the trellis design.

Materials

30 × 30 cm (12 × 12 in) 14 mesh regular mono canvas. Finished size is 20 cm (8½ in) square.

Crewel wool:
1 hank Flamingo 1
1 hank Chocolate 1 and 3,
1 hank White
2 × 20 Tapestry needles (easier to work the two shades for trellis)

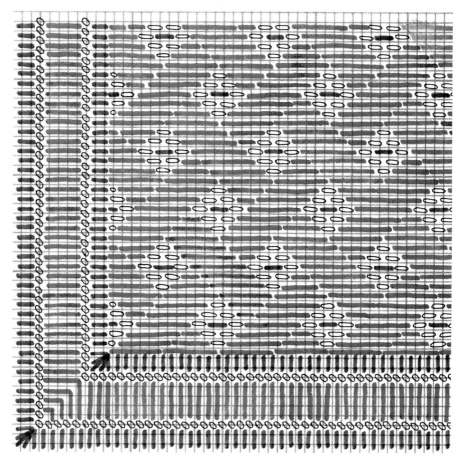

14

Stitches to refer to in Stitch index:
Straight Gobelin over 2 threads
Straight Gobelin over 4 threads
Continental Tent

Work trellis bars first, starting at the spot on the chart. The easiest way is to have 4 strands of Flamingo 1 in one needle and 4 strands of Chocolate 1 in the other and work the two colours alternately, following the chart. The small White stitches and single Chocolate 3 stitch can be worked later.

Finally, work the border starting in each corner (so they are all matching) and work an extra large group in the centre of each side as shown in the photograph.

Herb sachets and pincushions

These pieces are a delight to work. **Boxes** has a *Rhodes* stitch in the centre—one of the most spectacular canvas stitches—and around it is worked a very simple but very smooth *Straight Gobelin* and two widths of satin ribbon both stitched and couched.

The **Lattice** design is worked on finer canvas and has the wide ribbon couched on the diagonal and the spaces have *Eyelet* and *2468-tie stitches* worked in them; a simple Florentine border worked in pearl and stranded cotton completes it.

Boxes

Materials

20×20 cm ($7\frac{3}{4} \times 7\frac{3}{4}$ in) 14 mesh white mono canvas. Finished size is 15 cm (6 in) square.
Crewel wool:
  $\frac{1}{2}$ hank each Chocolate 1 and 3
  1 small skein Flamingo 1
  $\frac{1}{2}$ hank Flame 5
Double faced satin ribbon:
  $1\frac{1}{2}$ m ($1\frac{1}{2}$ yd) Cream 3 mm ($\frac{1}{10}$ in) wide
  1 m ($1\frac{1}{4}$ yd) Sable 1.5 mm ($\frac{1}{20}$ in) wide
  1 m ($1\frac{1}{4}$ yd) Peach 1.5 mm ($\frac{1}{20}$ in) wide

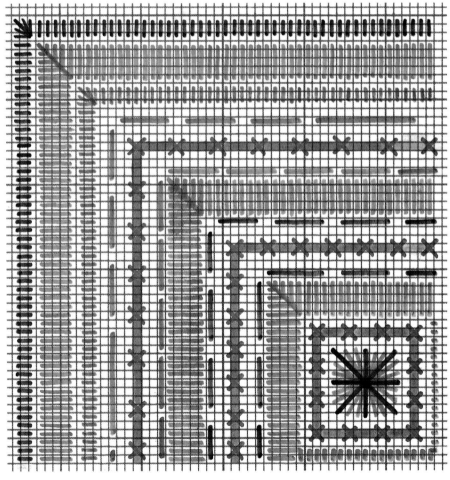

Stitches to refer to in Stitch index:
Rhodes
Straight Gobelin over 2
Straight Gobelin over 4
Cross

Start in the centre with a *Rhodes stitch* (3 strands crewel) and work outwards using 4 strands of crewel for all *Straight Gobelin* and 1 strand only for the *Cross stitch* to hold the ribbon.

Stitch the narrow ribbon, keeping it as smooth as possible. Couch down wide ribbon and at each corner turn it over and hold with a *Cross stitch*.

To start and finish the wide ribbon, simply overlap about 2 cm ($\frac{3}{4}$ in) along the final side and stitch over the two ends. Do not try to take it through the canvas.

Lattice—herb sachet

Materials

20 × 20 cm (7¾ in) white 18 mesh regular mono canvas. Finished size is 14 cm (5½ in) square.

DMC pearl cotton no 5:
  1 skein each Coral 754 and 948 and White
DMC stranded cotton:
  2 skeins Mouline 353
  1 skein Mouline 754
Double faced satin ribbon:
  1½ m (1½ yd) White, 3 mm (1/10 in) wide
  1½ m (1½ yd) Sable, 3 mm (1/10 in) wide

Stitches to refer to in Stitch index:

2458-tie	353 use 9 strands
Eyelet	754 (pearl) use 1 strand
Cross	948 use 1 strand
Upright Cross	948 use 1 strand
Backstitch	948 use 1 strand

Working on a frame, set up the diagonals with the two colours of ribbon; they weave over and under each other and are caught at each intersection with an upright cross. (It is easier and more economical to lay a long piece of ribbon, take it through to the back of the canvas and then cut it, rather than to

Centre

try and cut accurate lengths in advance.) It may help pass the ribbon through by enlarging the canvas hole slightly with the point of small embroidery scissors.

Following chart, work *Eyelets* and *2468-tie* stitches, in the colours and threads listed above. Work *Satin stitch* in the half diamonds around the edge—use 1 strand pearl cotton 948. The stitch count is 1, 2, 3, 4, 5, 4, 3, 2, 1.

Work Florentine border following chart with 9 strands of 353 and 754 stranded cotton. Fill in top and bottom with 1 thread white pearl cotton. Work *Cross*

stitch around edge. Finally, work *Backstitch* between border and lattice with 1 strand 948 pearl cotton.

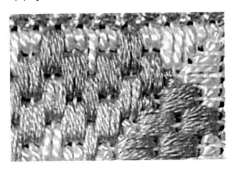

Needlepoint in upholstery

A set of dining chairs would be a really generous present. Indeed, what would be nicer than for a group of people to get together and stitch a set of Florentine seat covers for a friend's wedding anniversary.

Most Florentine patterns are suitable for upholstery and there are six further designs shown on page 25. However, avoid patterns with very long stitches which might snag and do not choose too coarse a canvas mesh: none of the patterns here have any stitches longer than 6 canvas threads and 14 mesh canvas is used.

Always watch the back of the work. It is very easy to find some areas have short stitches behind the work and others have long stitches. This happens particularly with 'valley and peak' designs such as the flash up the side of the slippers on page 36, but even when working the curve of the lozenge on the dining chair one is apt to have short stitches behind when stitching up the curve and long ones when coming down. It is important to be consistent, and when hard wear is required from a piece long stitches are needed behind the work.

Florentine is a good choice for a set of chairs for several reasons. It is relatively quick to work compared with a pictorial flower design worked in *Tent stitch*; unlike following a chart or counting out a geometric pattern it is fairly sociable, and once the first pattern repeat is on the canvas it is simple to follow it until the canvas is complete.

Florentine patterns can also be varied in many interesting ways, a great advantage when planning such a big project. This chair is one of a pair that will be worked identically; the other two in the set of four will have the colours reversed so the lozenge outlines will become lighter and the flowers dark.

If the set of chairs includes carvers with arms it would be particularly attractive to design a monogram to be worked in the centre of each seat. For this design omit the outline for five flowers and four diamond shapes and work the monogram in with a background of *Diagonal Tent*.

The two main types of chairs are those with drop-in seats and those that are upholstered-over. There is generally much less work to be done if they are the drop-in variety. However, preparation of the canvas is much the same. For the drop-in, measure the width across the front rail, as well as the back (frequently narrower) and then measure the depth, front to back dimension. Cut the canvas allowing an extra 7 cm (3 in) on all sides. Mark the area to be worked with pencil or tacking thread, allowing for the wooden frame of the seat just to cover the stitched area. With an upholstered-over chair a fabric template will help as there may well be a fold on the front two corners that will not need to be worked and frequently there are flaps that go between the rungs of the chair back which will have to be worked. But here again, cut canvas to the greatest measure in both directions allowing an extra 7 cm (3 in) all round. In both instances do not trim or shape the canvas—let the upholsterer cut where necessary when he is doing the final fixing.

When calculating the amount of wool to buy for a big project, either test stitch one pattern and multiply the yarn used or, more simply, if more than one seat is being worked, divide the wool for each seat before starting the first so there will be enough for each. At the end of the first check any extra wool that may be needed.

Never start a seat with too little wool to finish it—variations between seat covers will hardly show, but a change in the middle of the pattern will be very obvious.

If, however, disaster strikes and the wool runs out, here are tips for making the best of it. Keep a note of the colour numbers being used. Take unstitched wool

to match—stitching seems to change colour. Get extra wool in good time, not when down to the last thread. Mix 1 thread of the new dye lot with 3 old for a needle or two, then 2 plus 2 and so on until a full needle of new thread is used.

To make the overall pattern balance symmetrically on the finished project, start a motif in the centre of the canvas.

One last tip with the drop-in variety of chair seat. Do let the upholsterer see the chair frame before starting his job, as needlepoint can be thicker than ordinary fabric and occasionally the seat frame needs to be trimmed very slightly in order to take the extra thickness. One can only tell by examining how snugly the seat drops into the chair frame.

Florentine chair seat

When choosing the needlepoint pattern for the chairs, look at their style. This distinctive pattern looks well on bold or antique chairs but there is a selection of Florentine patterns on page 25, to suit most styles of chair.

Bargello Stars (Cornflower and Green) would also look good in fairly large areas but is more suited to feminine chairs like Victorian balloon backs or a bedroom stool.

Trellis, shown on page 14, **Pears** (Cornflower and Flamingo), and **Petite Fleur** (Chocolate and Flamingo) are all so versatile that they would be good designs for any type of chair.

Kell's Patchwork in White and Flamingo would be very pretty in a country dining room or alcove.

Garlands with the *Straight Gobelin* background as shown would again be lovely for a bedroom stool or chair; with a *Skip Cross stitch* background it makes a lovely cushion.

Ribbons would be a beautiful border on a square squab seat or stool.

This chair seat which has approximately 2,500 sq. cm (320 sq. in) of stitching took 7½ hanks crewel wool but it is well worth referring to the notes on calculating quantities at the beginning of this section; a short time spent on test stitching a pattern can avoid a great deal of trouble later on.

Materials
14 mesh regular mono canvas cut to the largest dimensions plus 7 cm (3 in) all round
Crewel wool:
　2 hanks Coral 1, 2, and 4
　1½ hanks Coral 3

Mark the shape of the area to be stitched on to the canvas with pencil; in the case of a drop-in seat the edge of the stitching should go just beyond where the frame will cover it.

Start in the centre and work outwards balancing the pattern repeats on the sides and finishing off straight along the front and back edges.

There is no right or wrong order in the working of the piece but it is probably easiest to work all the outlines first and then fill in each area with the flowers etc.

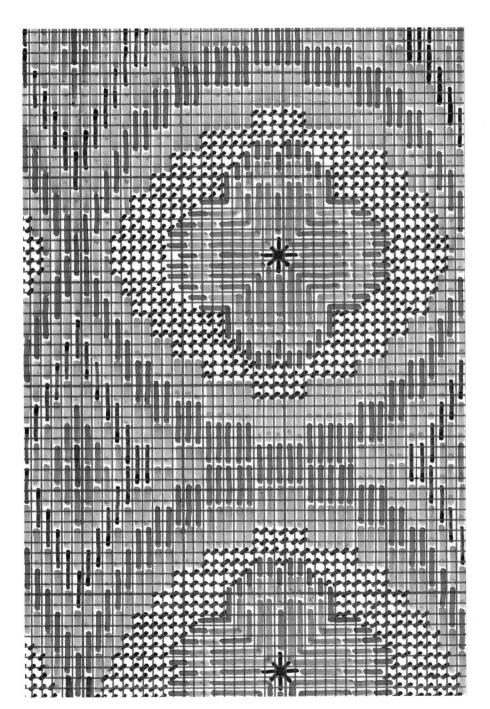

23

Florentine curtain tie back

To make a tie back, it is necessary to cut a template to determine the most attractive length. Curtains with a simple lining and a single width in the drop will obviously need a shorter tie back than those with heavy interlinings and two or three widths. If a generous drape is required, a longer tie back will be needed than one for catching back a narrow column of fabric.

The pattern used here is similar to the dining chair pattern but both the count of the outline lozenge and the flower are slightly different. Both patterns could be used equally well; the carved roundels on the chair splats suggested the small adaptation.

On the opposite page, a number of other designs are stitched, all of which would be ideal for working on upholstery pieces. See page 22 for other uses.

Materials

All tie backs will vary in length. This was worked on 18 mesh interlock canvas and used 1 hank each of Chocolate 1 and 3, Flamingo 1 and Coral 1.

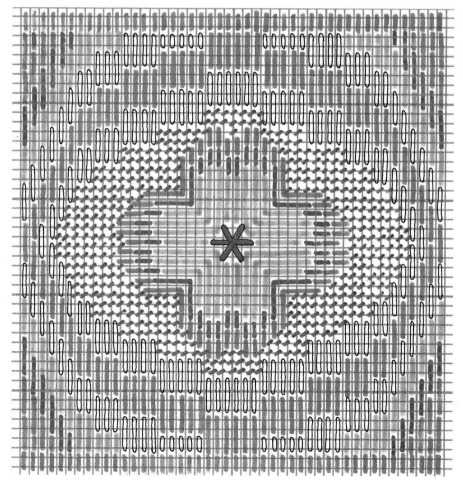

Designs for upholstery

Petite Fleur

Bargello Stars

Kell's Patchwork

Pears

Ribbons

Garlands

Presents for her

Bags, belts and handbag accessories are great fun to make and both useful and beautiful. Bags and co-ordinating belts are almost impossible to find other than in plain leather, and for 'after six' everything is covered with diamante or can only be found in the designer boutiques.

Spectacle cases, cheque book covers, credit card holders, key rings or even a cover for a small note pad are all tremendously useful; they can be in bright colours, to be noticed at a glance, or in smart deep colours—either way, they can frequently be made from leftover bits.

There are three types of bag in this section. The first is pre-finished—it arrives complete with a removable panel, where pieces of needlepoint, embroidery or even dress fabric can be fitted. The second has the front and back panels worked. The third one, photographed with a collection of belts, has just the front panel worked, the back is made out of dark grey gros grain fabric.

Evening bag

This bag is made in black suede and calf or in navy calf and has a panel which can be covered with needlepoint or embroidery to match different outfits. It makes an elegant present in itself and more panels could be added later to make it a most useful bag.

There are two panels in the photograph—**Trellis** (chart on page 14) worked without the border and **Petite Fleur** (on page 23), another versatile Florentine pattern which has been suggested for some of the other projects.

For additional panels why not try one or more of the initials from pages 62/63 or make up an interwoven monogram using the desired letters. Ribbons would be beautiful, either stitched in the **Trellis** design or couched in a lattice design similar to the herb sachet on page 18.

Materials

30 × 20 cm (12 × 7¾ in) 18 mesh regular mono canvas. This will do for either panel.

Trellis

DMC stranded cotton:
  6 skeins 738 and 739 Dark and Light Champagne
  4 skeins Black
Metallic Balger Gold 16: 1 skein

Petite Fleur

DMC stranded cotton:
  6 skeins Ecru
  6 skeins 3687 and 3688 Dark and Light Mulberry
Metallic Balger Silver 16: 1 skein

Working either panel

Use 8 strands stranded cotton and 1 thread Balger.

Work panel so that it is about ⅔ cm (¼ in) larger than the area cut out of the bag in both directions. When complete, trim canvas to about 8 threads away from work, turn the spare canvas to the back and slip stitch in place.

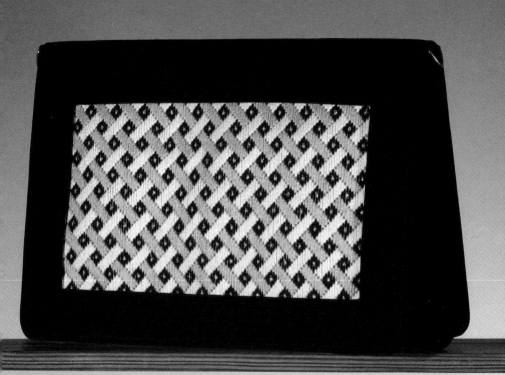

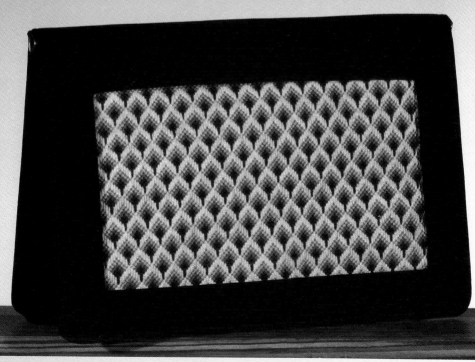

Spectacle case

The front only was worked

Materials

15 × 25 cm (6 × 10 in) 14 mesh regular mono canvas. Finished size is 17 × 10 cm (6¾ × 4 in).
DMC stranded cotton: 2 hanks 311 Navy
DMC pearl cotton: 1 ball no 5 Ecru

Stitches to refer to in Stitch index:
Diagonal Tent

Use 9 strands stranded cotton and 2 strands pearl cotton for all stitching except the initial and its background. Use 6 strands for the initial and 1 for the *Diagonal Tent*.

If preferred the pattern can be continued on both sides of the case (like the bag on the next page). Alternatively the back could also be worked with the pattern, and initial only used on one side.

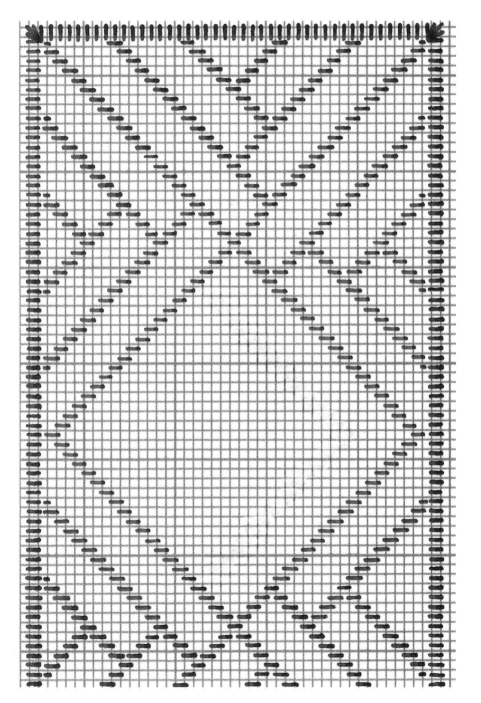

Navy and cream bag

This is the reverse colour scheme to the spectacle case on pages 28/29—more practical for a bag. Another combination that would look stunning is black crewel wool and gold thread instead of the cream.

The central diamond shape can be filled with an initial on one or both sides.

When making up the bag, side gussets will keep the neat line and give far more room for the contents inside. Gussets on spectacle cases are also a good idea.

Handles, shoulder straps or chains are also important to consider; a shoulder-hanging bag leaves your hands free and helps keep fingers off the needlework. Clips can be fitted inside the bag so a heavy gold-link chain can be slipped on when needed. The alternative, as shown here, is an old necklace—so often the clasp breaks. It is a good length and makes an unusual chain.

Materials

35 × 43 cm (14 × 17 in) 14 mesh regular mono canvas. Finished size of bag is 25 × 17 cm (10 × 6¾ in).

Crewel wool: 2 hanks Bright China Blue 8

DMC stranded cotton: 6 skeins Ecru

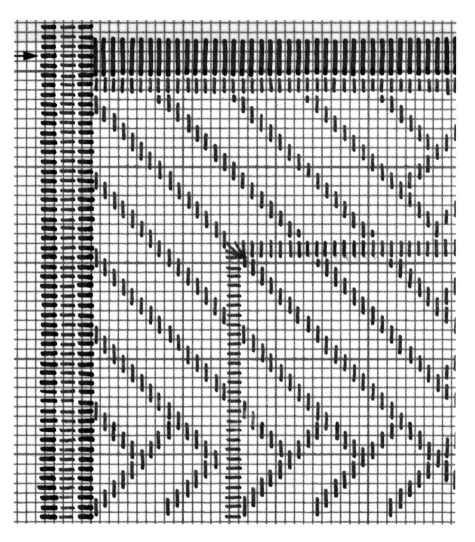

Stitches to refer to in Stitch index:

Straight Gobelin over 2 and over 4 threads
Four Crossed Corner and variations
Shell

Use 4 strands crewel and 9 strands stranded cotton except for the *Shell stitch* (only 6 strands).

Only the front flap of the bag is shown in the chart. The row of *Straight Gobelin* over 4 threads marked with an arrow forms the central fold and should be worked across the centre of the short width of canvas first; then work front panel following chart. Turn both the canvas and chart upside-down and repeat for the back panel. N.B. When working with dark and light wools it is very important to bring the needle up in an empty hole and down in a hole that already has wool in it .

31

Belts and bags

Mix and match patterns are amusing to wear and even more fun to work out and stitch. Here is a bag with the front panel worked in columns of different patterns together with three belts, two of which repeat patterns used on the bag.

The belts also show three interesting ways of finishing: the top one is a series of octagonal pieces of plastic canvas, each worked with a star motif. When the edges are bound, a brass curtain ring is caught in at the centre of each side, and a ring attached at either end allows for the belt to be tied with a decorative cord. This project would be particularly suitable for a young person to make as the small pieces of canvas are so quick to work and the making-up happens as one stitches. How about putting a letter of the person's name in each square (alphabet on pages 60/61)?

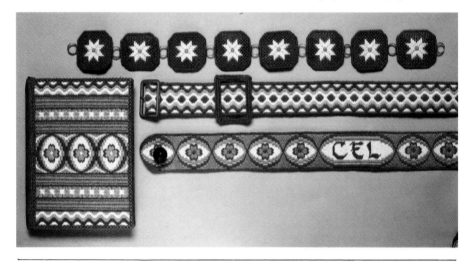

Lozenge belt

Materials
12 cm (4½ in) width by waist dimension plus 20 cm (7¾ in) 18 mesh regular mono canvas
Crewel wool:
  2 hanks Iron 3
  2 hanks White
  1 hank Iron 5

Mark final size on to canvas as explained opposite and work pattern from both ends towards centre; adapt the centre motif to fit the space available. Use 3 strands for all stitching except the *Diagonal Tent* which needs only 2 strands. When complete, stitch 2 rows of *Tent stitch* in dark grey

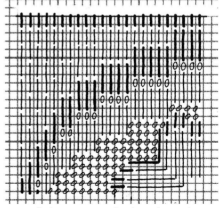

around the curves at both ends so that no canvas will show on the curve.

The number of canvas panels depends on the approximate waist size. However, if you were planning to stitch a name, the letters could always be spaced out, with plain panels in between, if necessary.

The belt with the **Wave** pattern—simply one of the columns on the bag doubled— has a ready-made buckle but there are buckles that can be covered in your own fabric if preferred.

The final belt is dressier and looks best if it fits well. The easiest way to achieve a good fit with this pattern is to measure the waist, mark the canvas and start at both ends. Work the **Lozenge** patterns towards the central point and adapt the central motif (which will be worn centre back) to fit the space which is left.

Shop around for interesting cords to make the tie .

Wave belt

Materials

10 cm (4 in) width by waist dimension plus 20 cm ($7\frac{3}{4}$ in) 18 mesh regular mono canvas

Crewel wool:

$1\frac{1}{2}$ hanks White

1 hank Iron 3 and Iron 5

Use 3 strands wool throughout.

Following chart work white 'spots' down central line of canvas. Continue to work outwards with colours as shown.

Before working the compensation stitches adjust design as necessary to fit (shown hollow on the chart) buckle.

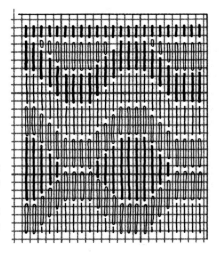

Star octagonal belt

Materials

Panel 10 mesh plastic canvas

Crewel wool:

1 hank White

1 hank Iron 5

Brass curtain rings

Cut the canvas into octagons 24 threads by 24 threads with corners cut off as in the chart (cut them all in the same direction). Each piece measures approximately 6 cm ($2\frac{1}{4}$ in) square and the ring makes a space of about 2 cm ($\frac{3}{4}$ in) between each piece; so work seven pieces for a 60 cm (23 in) waist.

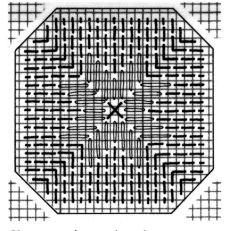

Use 4 strands crewel wool .

Co-ordinating bag

The front panel of this bag incorporates the **Lozenge** and **Wave** patterns from two of the belts.

Working any project with columns of stitches is a good way of making an original design. Here the widest and boldest pattern was worked down the centre. This was balanced by simple *Knitting*, then a column of *Reversed Eyelet*, *Knitting* again and finally the Florentine **Wave** pattern. In between each column is a single row of *Cross stitch* in the dark grey. In this way the five busy columns with the plain *Knitting* in between make an attractive design.

Materials

35 × 25 cm (14 × 10 in) 18 mesh regular mono canvas. Finished size of bag is 25 × 18½ cm (10 × 7½ in).

Crewel wool:
1 hank each White and Iron 3
1½ hanks Iron 1

Stitches to refer to in Stitch index:
Cross stitch
Crossed Corners
Knitting
Reversed Eyelet and *Rhodes*
Diagonal Tent

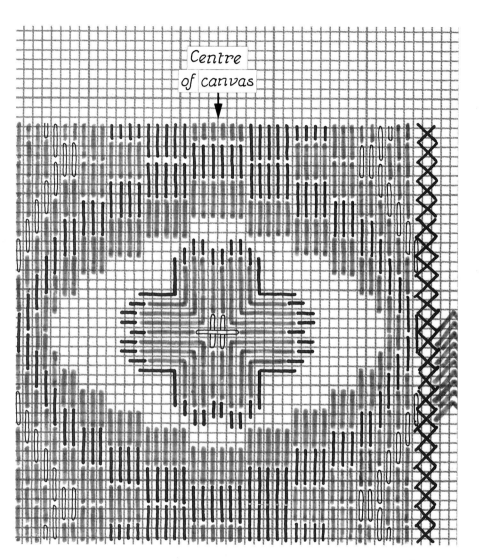

Centre
of canvas

Find the centre of the canvas and mark the canvas outwards over 22, 2, 12, 2, 12, 2, 12, 2, 12 and 4 threads.

Work *Cross* in dark grey over 2 threads.

Work the central **Lozenge** panel following the chart using 3 strands for flowers and upright Florentine stitches, 2 strands for the *Tent*.

Work 4 columns of *Knitting* with 2 strands Iron 1, *Backstitch* alternate rows with 1 strand Iron 3. Work *Reversed Eyelet* (2 strands Iron 1) with *Rhodes* (2 strands White). Work both **Wave** columns using 3 strands crewel.

Finally work row of *Crossed Corners* on all four sides of panel using 2 strands Iron 1 for base cross and 2 strands Iron 3 for tipping the arms.

35

Presents for him

There are several things in this book that would be ideal presents for men if stitched in masculine colours. The spectacle case shown on page 28 but stitched in burgundy and dark grey, and the round box on page 53 for his cuff-links, would be splendid gifts.

Slippers

These shoes or slippers are beautifully finished with leather insides and proper soles. They are not things one can make up oneself and they do have to fit—therefore, do find a bootmaker who will undertake the finishing for you. Ask for a template for the size and area which is to be stitched.

Two alternative patterns for the front are included on the chart.

Materials

45 × 56 cm (18 × 22 in) 18 mesh regular mono canvas for a pair of size 9 shoes
Crewel wool:
  1 hank Cornflower 1
  1 hank Bright China Blue 3, 5 and 9
  1 hank Chocolate 3

Mark canvas from template. Start the Florentine pattern at the arrow on the chart, 12 cm (4½ in) from the top of the tongue; using 3 strands crewel wool work out to the left continuing the pattern until the side is reached. Follow the colour sequence shown and balance the pattern on the right-hand side of the shoe. Continue the same colour sequence down the canvas. Work initial(s) of your choice in navy *Continental Tent stitch* and work *Diagonal Tent* on the background (2 strands).

36

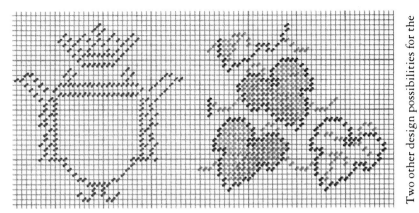

Chess-board

The chess-board is worked on 18 mesh canvas; do check the size of the chess-men before starting work as some are so big they would look better on a board worked on 14 mesh canvas (each square would be slightly bigger).

The border has pulled thread stitches and must be worked on a frame. For a less complicated edge, work simple rows of *Straight Gobelin*.

The pulled thread stitch would also look lovely worked around an initial (it might be easier to work the border and then ·centre the letter in the space which is left).

Materials

50 × 50 cm (20 × 20 in) 18 mesh regular mono canvas

Crewel wool:
  1½ hanks Brown Grounding 7
Lyscord cotton:
  1 ball no 3 Beige 22
  1 ball Off-white 21
Needles: 1 each 20 and 22 Tapestry

Find the centre of canvas by folding. Mark squares over 24 threads with pencil or tacking thread. Mark border over 2, then 22, then 4 threads. Mount on frame.

A	B.ₐ	D	C	
	A	B.ₐ	D	C
B.ᵦ		A	B.ₐ	D
	B.ᵦ	A	B.ₐ	D
C		B.ᵦ	A	B.ₐ
	C	B.ᵦ	A	B.ₐ
D	C	B.ᵦ	A	
	D	C	B.ᵦ	A

Using the 22 Tapestry needle, work all cream squares with 1 strand Lyscord. Make absolutely sure that the waste knot is in the line of stitching and does not trail behind an area that will be left exposed. Note that there are extra long stitches on two sides of the D squares. Start with a diagonal row of squares marked A (upper left-hand corner in the chart). Within the square, start the stitch in the upper left-hand corner.

Then work squares marked Ba: start these squares in lower left-hand corner; work up with horizontal stitches and down with vertical ones.

Then work Bb: start in lower left-hand corner and work up and down diagonally.

Then work C: start in lower left-hand corner and count carefully.

Finally, work D: note that the *Straight Gobelin* is over 3 threads along bottom and right-hand side.

Work all remaining squares (not labelled on diagram) in 2 strands crewel wool in *Cushion stitch* over 4 threads.

Work border starting on the inside edge with the *Straight Gobelin* over 2 threads; work all the solid stitches in the Brown crewel and Beige Lyscord: use 3 strands crewel and 1 Lyscord. Finally, using the size 20 needle, work the pulled thread stitches following the numbers on the chart with 1 strand Off-white Lyscord.

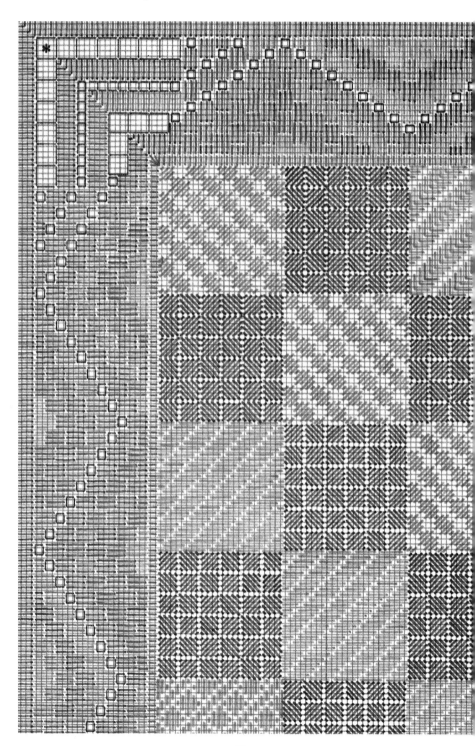

*Pulled thread stitches

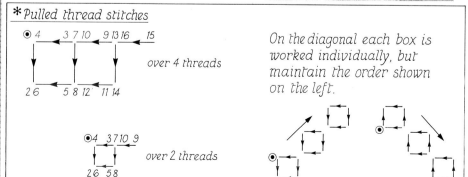

⊙ 4   3 7 10 9 13 16 15

over 4 threads

2 6   5 8 12' 11 14

On the diagonal each box is worked individually, but maintain the order shown on the left.

⊙4 3 7 10 9

over 2 threads

2 6 5 8

41

Small gifts

Here is a selection of tiny gifts for the
occasion when something small is needed
to show appreciation or to say 'Thank you'.
Perhaps a friend is moving away to a new
area, or a night is spent as a house-guest.
People love to be thought of and a small
piece of stitching is the perfect solution.
Dressing the Christmas tree with stitched
decorations also gives a much more personal flavour to such a festive occasion.

These small things are great fun to think
up and quick to work; any leftover 'bits'
and canvas off-cuts can be put to good
purpose in this way.

Keep all started skeins (the same dye lot
might be difficult to find), short pieces of
metallics, cords, braid, sequin waste,
beads, knitting wools, in fact anything
that might work on canvas. There is no
need to remember where they have come
from or worry about not getting them
again as the projects are so small they will
only take a length or two; they just have to
look right.

Christmas ornaments

Tie tag

Materials
16 × 16 threads 7 mesh plastic canvas
Red and green wool

Cut a hole 3 threads square 3 threads in
from the top right-hand corner. Use 3
strands wool for the *Tent* and *Cushion stitch*,
and 4 strands for the *Binding stitch*.

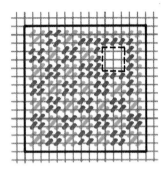

Napkin ring

Materials
16 × 68 threads 10 mesh plastic canvas
Red and green wool

Use 3 strands red and green wool for
Cushion stitch. Use 3 strands red for the
Braided Cross stitch and use 4 strands red for
the *Binding stitch*.

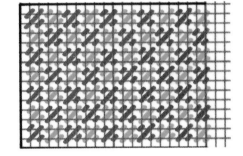

Matchbox

Materials
A small piece of 16 mesh gold sprayed regular
    mono canvas
DMC stranded cotton:
    Green 701
    Red 606
    Use 6 strands throughout

The *Vertical Cross stitch* is across 2 threads
and up 4 threads. When complete, trim
canvas to 2 threads on all sides. Pull 1
thread off on each to 'fringe' the panel and
stick to matchbox which has already been
covered with felt or paper.

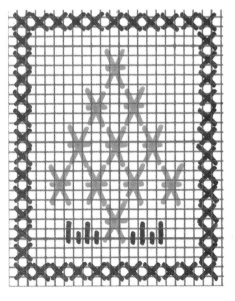

Boxes

The easiest way to work the panels of this box is to complete the stitching before cutting the individual side panels. There are 2 threads between each panel and 1 thread around the edge.

Materials

50 × 44 threads 10 mesh plastic canvas
Red wool (4 strands)
Metallic:
Twilleys Double Goldfingering (1 strand)
1 m (1¼ yd) Offray 1.5 mm (1/20 in) red ribbon

Chart A shows how to place the panels on the canvas. Work panels 1 and 2 following Chart B for top and bottom of box. *Straight Gobelin* stitch has been used throughout.

Work panels 3 and 4 twice following Chart C.

Join all sides with *Binding stitch* in 4 strands red wool and thread narrow red ribbon through *Straight Gobelin stitch* as if wrapping a parcel and finish with bow.

Sew on loop made with the red wool if you wish to hang the box from the Christmas tree.

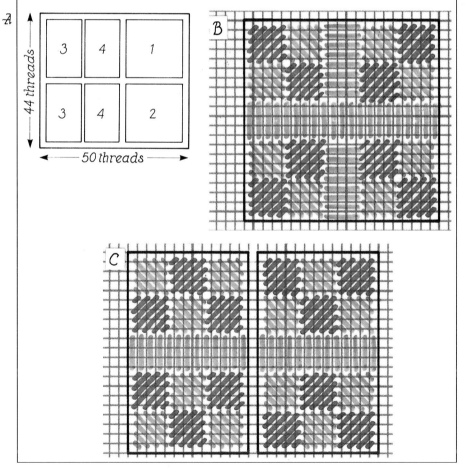

Table settings

Your guests will remember that special meal for a long time, particularly if their initials are stitched on the matchboxes; they would make wonderful gifts.

The napkin ring, coaster and tie tag are made on plastic canvas. While the exact sizes that are photographed here have been given, it would be an easy matter to enlarge or reduce the ring if the napkins are bulky. The Easter coaster has the same chicken as on the napkin ring but it is worked on 7 mesh canvas rather than 10 to make it larger.

The matchbox front was stitched on fine interlock canvas.

When working small projects, it is easier to work on a reasonable piece of canvas, and to trim it to the right size afterwards. Either use interlock canvas of the specified mesh if available (it does not fray) or run colourless nail varnish around the back edges as soon as it is trimmed.

Coasters

The Easter coaster could have a hole cut in it above the chicken's tail and become a tie tag.

Materials
20 × 20 thread 7 mesh plastic canvas
Crewel wool: yellow, orange, green and white
Use 4 strands for *Tent* stitch
Use 5 threads for *Binding stitch*

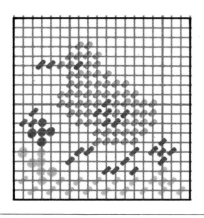

Easter matchbox

Materials
48 × 26 thread 14 mesh interlock canvas
Crewel wool: yellow, orange and green
White pearl cotton for background
Use 3 strands crewel wool throughout and 1 strand pearl cotton.
The stitches used are *Tent* with a row of *Cushion* around the edge.

When making up, trim canvas right up to design, run colourless nail varnish or clear glue on back edges and stick to front of prepared matchbox.

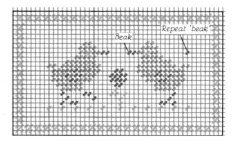

Easter napkin ring

Materials
18 × 68 thread 10 mesh plastic canvas
Crewel wool: yellow, orange, green and white
Use 3 strands for *Tent stitch*
3 strands for *Braided cross*

4 strands for *Binding stitch*

There is a single hollow stitch on the matchbox front cover. This is the first stitch of the chicken's beak for the continuous row for the ring. Five chickens will fit if done this way.

Bookmarks

Perforated paper has been used for these two projects. Once very popular with Victorian embroiderers, it has recently reappeared on the market. Tips for working with it are given in the introduction. In both cases the bookmarks were mounted on wide ribbon bonded on the back of the 'canvas' with *Bondaweb*—an iron-on *Vilene* that cuts out stitching. The pale pink used behind the **Bows** was just narrow enough not to show and the edge of the perforated paper was carefully trimmed with pinking shears. One sheet makes three bookmarks.

The **Ladybirds** have an edging of wide red ribbon which becomes part of the overall design.

Bows

Materials
Perforated paper
DMC stranded cotton:
  1 skein each of Green 906
  Pink 899
  Yellow 445
  Use 4 strands
1 m (1¼ yd) Offray 1.5 mm ($\frac{1}{20}$ in) green ribbon
Wide pink ribbon

Follow chart in *Cross stitch* over 1 thread. The arrows show the pattern repeat.

Cut the ribbon in half and couch each half down one side of the design with *Cross stitch* over 2 threads worked in pink. Overlap the ribbons at the top and bottom (as shown in chart) and work a *Cross stitch* over the two ribbons to secure them.

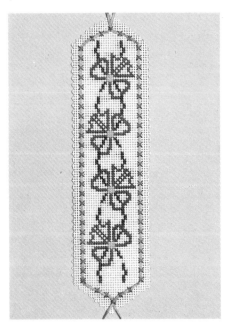

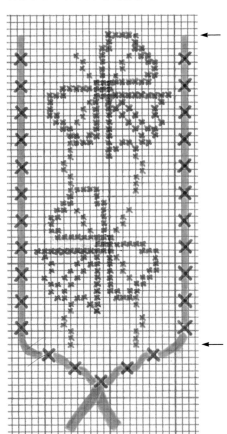

48

Ladybirds

Materials

Perforated paper

DMC stranded cotton:
  1 skein each of Red 606
  Black 310
  Use 4 strands

Metallic:
  1 skein Twilley's Goldfingering WG 34 red
  1 m ($1\frac{1}{4}$ yd) Offray 1.5 mm ($\frac{1}{20}$ in) red ribbon

Wide red ribbon

Stitches to refer to in Stitch index:
  Cross stitch
  Skip Cross stitch

Follow chart, spacing ladybirds out as shown. Work them in *Cross stitch* over 1 thread. Work initial in *Cross stitch* over 1 thread. Thread narrow ribbon and lay it, in turn, along each edge and take through the corner hole to the back and trim. Couch the ribbon with *Cross stitch* over 2 threads. Work background in 1 strand metallic in *Skip Cross stitch*. Trim and mount on wide red ribbon.

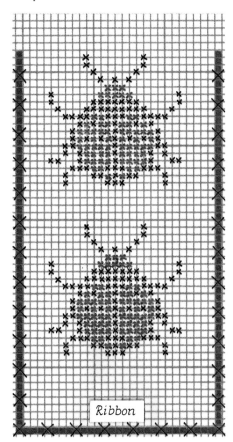

Ribbon

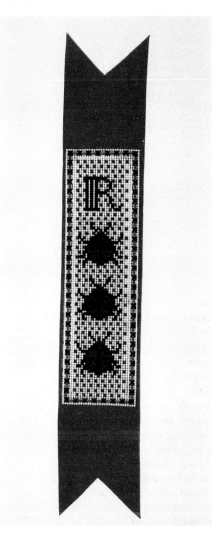

49

Packing the present

Jewellery casket

Finished size 10 × 10 × 10 cm (4 × 4 × 4 in)

Materials

2 × 11 cm (4¼ in) circular plastic pieces
7 mesh plastic canvas:
  1 top 27 × 40 threads
  1 back 27 × 14 threads
  1 front 27 × 14 threads
  1 base 27 × 25 threads
  2 sides 25 × 14 threads
  2 hinges 3 × 8 threads
Crewel wool:
  1 hank each Flamingo 1 and 2
  ½ hank Grass Green 1
  Use 4 strands

Stitches to refer to in Stitch index:
  Knitting
  Tent
  Straight Gobelin
  Backstitch
  Binding stitch

Top. Trim as diagram to form front closure and work piece, leaving unworked threads (top left and right) as shown for hinges to overlap. Note the reverse angle of *Tent stitch* on the right-hand side. Use pale Flamingo for *Knitting stitch* and *Tent*, deeper Flamingo for *Straight Gobelin* down centre. *Backstitch* either side of the *Straight Gobelin* with green. Overcast edge with closure using deeper Flamingo.
Back. Work as **Top** leaving unworked threads for hinges. Overlay the small hinges over the unworked area on the trunk top and unworked area on the back; work *Tent stitch* in deeper Flamingo through both pieces (this is easier if they are laid on a flat surface as they do not slip around). With same Flamingo, work *Binding stitch* along the back between hinges.
Domed area of casket lid. Cut the two

circular panels across the centre, immediately below the straight central thread. (These circles have a straight central thread one way and a more jagged one the other.) Trim 3 threads off outer edge of curve; work both pieces with pale Flamingo over 2 threads - more than one stitch may have to go into the same hole to cover the canvas well. With deeper Flamingo overcast straight edge of each half circle; join the curved edge to the top to form the top.
Base. Work in pale Flamingo *Diagonal Tent.*
Front. Work as the back.
Two ends. Work in *Knitting stitch* with three deep Flamingo *Tent stitches* in each corner.
  Join all the panels together with *Binding stitch* with deep Flamingo in the following order—front to sides; sides to back; base to sides; then overcast around the top of the panels. Finally make loop for flap.

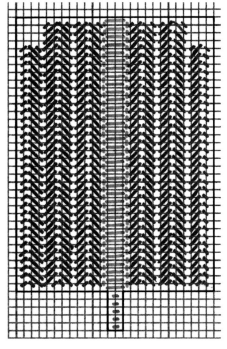

Blue flower box

Finished size 15 × 11 × 7 cm (6 × 4¼ × 3 in)

Materials
7 mesh plastic canvas:
  1 top 30 × 42 threads
  2 top sides 42 × 5 threads
  2 top ends 30 × 5 threads
  1 bottom 40 × 28 threads
  2 bottom sides 40 × 18 threads
  2 bottom ends 28 × 18 threads
Crewel wool:
  1 oz White (for background)
  ½ oz Bright Yellow 1 (for middle of flowers)
  1 oz Cornflower no 1 (for flowers)
  1 oz Bright China Blue (for overcasting)
  6 strands of wool were used throughout

Stitches to refer to in Stitch index:
Diagonal Tent
Binding stitch

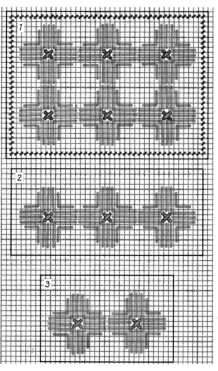

Lid. Work top following diagram. Complete background with *Diagonal Tent stitch* in White and finish with a row of deeper Blue *Tent stitch* 1 thread in from the edge. Work top sides and top ends in White *Diagonal Tent*.
Box. Work two long sides following diagram 2. Complete background in White (leaving the final thread on all edges for making up). Work two short sides following diagram 3. N.B. On these four panels the flowers are worked closer to the bottom in order to make them appear in the middle when the lid is on.
Base. Work base in *Diagonal Tent* in Blue.

Making up
Lid. Using the deeper Blue and the *Binding stitch*, join sides to top; overcast lower edge of lid. Join the sides with White.
Box. Bind the sides together with White and base to sides with Blue. Overcast the top edges with deep Blue.

Pencil tidy

Finished size 13 × 26 cm (5 × 10½ in)

Materials
35 × 66 thread 7 mesh plastic canvas
Do check that the canister is the right size
Crewel wool:
  1 hank White
  ½ hank each Bright Yellow, Cornflower and
    Bright China Blue

Start following the chart at the right-hand end of the canvas; there will be two rows of large flowers, five in each row for this size canister.
  Use 5 strands for flower petals and 4 strands for *Tent* and *Cross stitches*.
  Join the two ends with *Binding stitch*. Overcast the top and bottom edges.

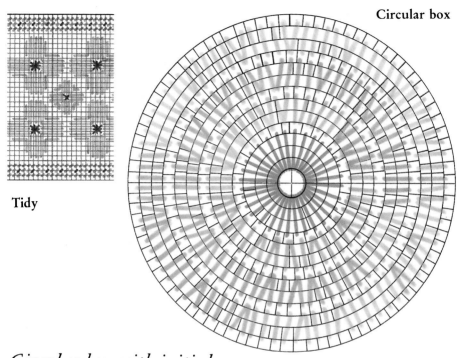

Circular box

Tidy

Circular box with initials

Finished size 8 cm ($3\frac{1}{4}$ in) diameter, 7 cm (3 in) deep

Materials

2 × 11 cm ($4\frac{1}{4}$ in) circular plastic canvas pieces

7 mesh plastic canvas:

   1 top side 66 × 4 threads

   1 top seam 5 × 2 threads

   1 bottom side 61 × 19 threads

   1 bottom seam 5 × 10 threads

Crewel wool:

   1 oz Bright Yellow no 1 for *Cushion stitch*

   $\frac{1}{2}$ oz Leaf Green or 1 small skein for initial

   $\frac{1}{2}$ oz Green for *Braided Cross* and *Binding stitch*

   6 strands of wool were used throughout

Stitches to refer to in Stitch index:

Cushion

Braided Cross

Binding stitch

Lid. Work circular top in *Straight stitch* with cross in centre following chart. Baste short ends of top side-piece together to form circle and then baste side seam-piece over seam on wrong side to reinforce seam.

Working through both pieces at seam and counting both seam threads as 1, work *Cushion stitch* over 2 threads compensating where necessary. Using *Braided Cross stitch*, join top side-piece to round top-piece.

Base. Select initials and work them centrally on bottom side in *Tent stitch*. Continue to work as top. Seam bottom side-piece in same manner as top. Work in rows of *Cushion stitch*. Join to bottom-piece same as top. Overcast top edge of bottom and bottom edge of lid.

Stitch index

1. All the stitches used in the book are explained fully in this section. A list of stitches included in each project has been given with the materials.

2. Each diagram has a circled dot which denotes the best starting place. If diagrams are numbered work UP with the odd numbers and DOWN with the even numbers; following these numbers will give the neatest result. Wherever possible bring the needle up in an empty hole and take it down through one with wool in it.

3. In each diagram a needle is drawn in to show the direction of the wool at the back of the work. However, always 'stab stitch', i.e., go down through the canvas and then, as a separate movement, come up through the canvas. This will prevent distortion of the canvas threads.
   Always watch the back of the work.

4. Occasionally compensation stitches have to be worked to get a straight edge; these have been drawn as hollow stitches when explanation was needed.

5. When working any form of *Cross stitch*, it is very important to work the top stitch of each cross on the same slant.

6. When working stitches that will leave some of the canvas uncovered, such as *Skip Cross* or *Lace Cross*, it is important to avoid any other threads trailing across the back of the area. Work areas to be covered first and be sure to anchor all threads in their own stitches. When working the open-work areas use the existing solid stitchery for anchoring new threads and for finishing off any ends; start a row of stitches with enough thread to finish it, as changing to a new thread in the middle of the line will spoil the appearance.

Tent stitch— Continental

This stitch covers 1 diagonal canvas thread from lower left to upper right and the needle passes under 2 vertical canvas threads travelling towards the left giving a long stitch behind the work. When working the second and subsequent rows follow the chart and maintain the long stitch behind the work. This stitch is only used for very small areas or a single row.

Tent stitch—Diagonal or Basketweave

Use this stitch for any background or reasonable area of tent stitch. This method gives a neat basketweave appearance on the back of the canvas and prevents distortion and pulling. It is worked diagonally from the top right corner and the work is not turned; the needle passes horizontally under 2 warp threads and vertically under 2 weft threads.

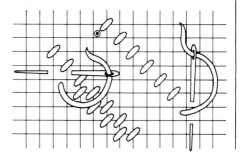

Binding stitch for plastic canvas

Use this stitch to bind all edges of plastic canvas projects.

Simply stitch the wool over and over the edge of the canvas covering one of the outside horizontal threads. At corners, go through the same hole two or three times to get good coverage. Trim any 'nubs' off the cut edges of the canvas before starting work and the stitch will lay more smoothly.

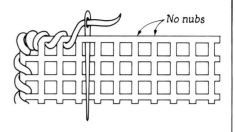

Braided Cross stitch for plastic canvas

Use this stitch to join two pieces of canvas together.

Sandwich the tail of the wool between the two layers of canvas so it will be caught by the stitching. Bring the needle through to the front in the first hole, go over the two layers to the back and come up through the third hole (leaving one free hole). Go to the back and come up through the first hole once more. Go over to the back and come through the fourth hole, then over and through the second hole.

Repeat using fifth and third holes, sixth and fourth holes and so on.

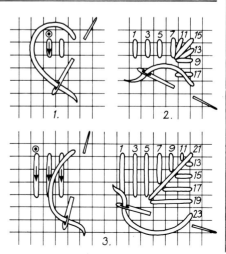

Straight Gobelin

This is a very versatile stitch that can easily be worked over 2, 3 or 4 or more threads of canvas.

When working a corner with *Straight Gobelin* over 2 threads follow (2) coming up on the odd numbers and going down five times into the corner pivot hole.

When working a larger-scale stitch, mitre the stitches into the corner, again coming up on the odd numbers, and working a final long stitch from the outer corner into the pivot hole. Continue along the next side as before.

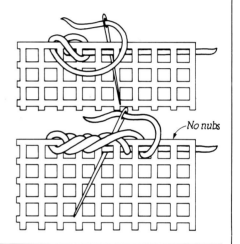

Cushion stitch

Another versatile stitch that can be worked to different scales. In this book it has been used over 2 threads (1) and 4 threads (2).

When using the small version work all the stitches at the same angle (1). When working over 4 threads, stitch two squares and then, with a contrasting colour lay a thread corner to corner (2) before working stitches on the other diagonal (3).

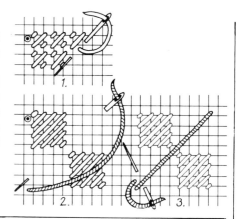

Diagonal Cross stitch

Work a half cross on the same slant for the whole area first; this slopes from upper left to lower right over 2 canvas threads and has a straight stitch behind the work (1). Work second half of cross following (2) which will give a long stitch behind the work for hard-wear and minimal distortion.

Diagram 3 shows area with top *Cross stitch* always on same slant.

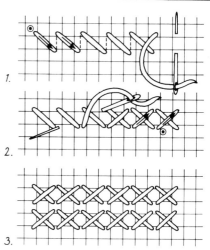

Upright Cross stitch

Work each complete cross in turn. Each stitch covers 2 threads of canvas and the horizontal stitch is worked last (1).

Diagram 2 shows how consecutive rows are worked.

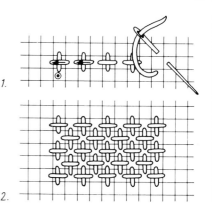

Crossed corners

Work large *Diagonal Cross stitch* over 4 threads of canvas first. Work a stitch over 2 threads of canvas diagonally over each point (1) and (2). These small stitches can be worked in a contrasting colour (3).

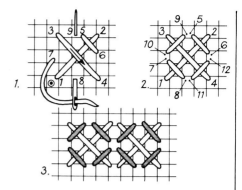

Skip Cross and Lace Cross

Refer to note 6 in the introduction.

For **Skip Cross** following (1) work from right to left covering 1 thread of canvas diagonally from upper right to lower left; the thread at the back of the work moves diagonally upwards to the left. When this

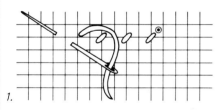

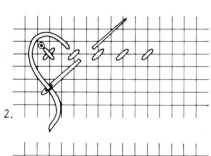

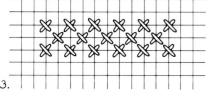

row is complete, follow (2) crossing the original stitches again with another short stitch behind the work.

Diagram 3 shows a completed area.

For **Lace Cross** following (1) start in top right-hand corner of area to be worked. Follow numbers carefully to ensure minimum thread (and bulk) behind work.

Diagram 2 shows how subsequent rows fit in: either reverse the stitches so there is still minimal thread behind the work or anchor off in the surrounding stitchery and start again at the right-hand margin.

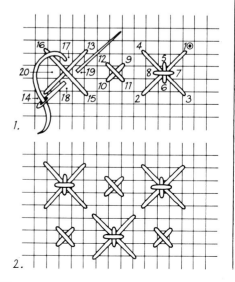

Shell stitch

Work a group of four upright stitches over 4 threads of canvas (A). Tie this bundle over 2 threads of canvas across the middle (note in diagram B how the stitches are pulled to one side).

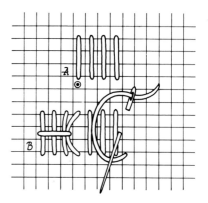

2468-tie stitch

Seven upright stitches are worked over 2, 4, 6, 8, 6, 4 and 2 threads to form a diamond. The central stitch can be tied in a contrast colour.

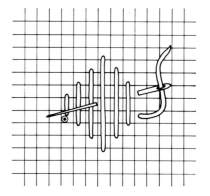

Eyelet stitch

Sixteen stitches worked down into the central hole. This stitch can easily be rescaled to cover 6, 10 or 12 threads.

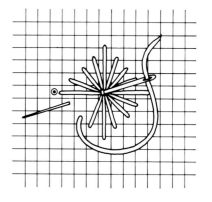

Knitting stitch and knitting with Backstitch variation

A diagonal stitch worked over 2 threads of canvas. It is worked in vertical rows up and down the canvas in alternate diagonal directions.

The hollow stitches shown at the top and bottom of the columns on the left are compensation stitches which will be necessary at the top and bottom of each row.

Diagram 2 shows the *Backstitch* worked on alternate rows.

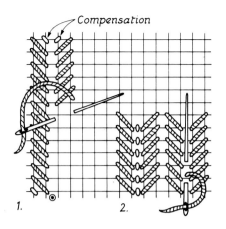

Compensation

1.

2.

Rhodes stitch

A bold stitch that uses a lot of wool. Always follow the numbers when stitching otherwise the last stitch might not be at the same angle and will look messy. This stitch can easily be re-scaled and worked over 4, 6, 8, 10 or 12 threads when needed.

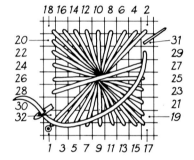

Reversed eyelet with Rhodes stitch

Work *Rhodes stitch* over 6 threads of canvas. For the *Reversed eyelet stitch* work four stitches down into a corner hole and then two stitches into the hole one short of the corner and finally two more stitches into the next hole.

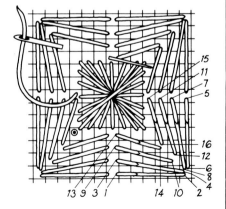

Alphabets

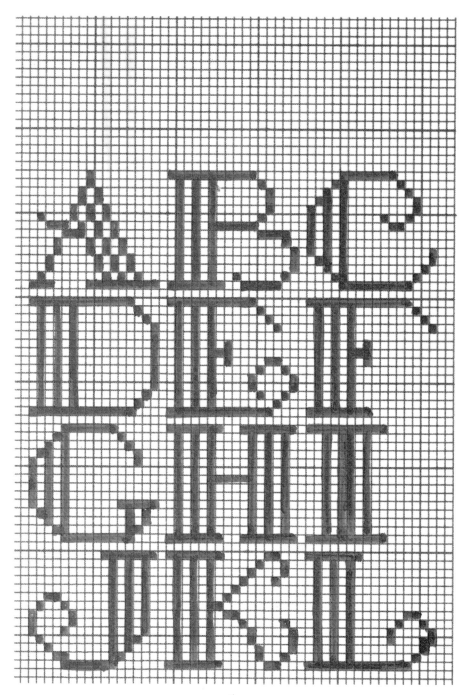

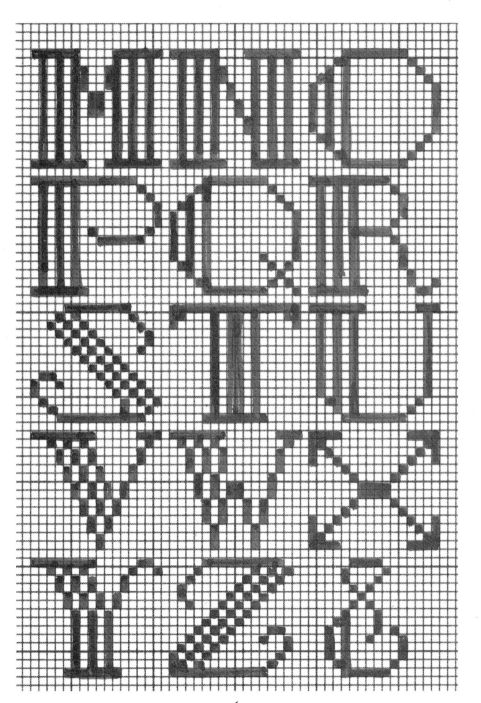

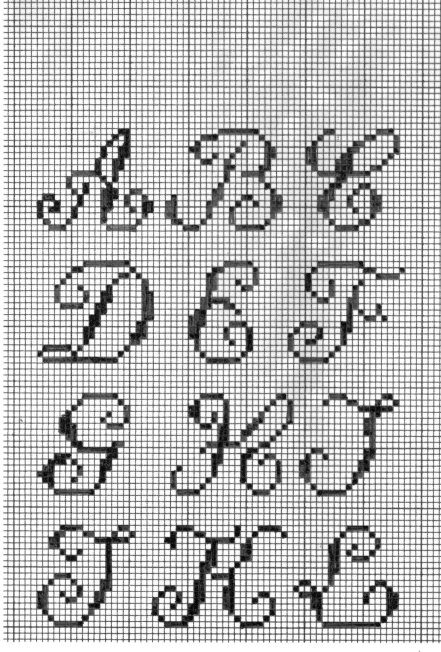

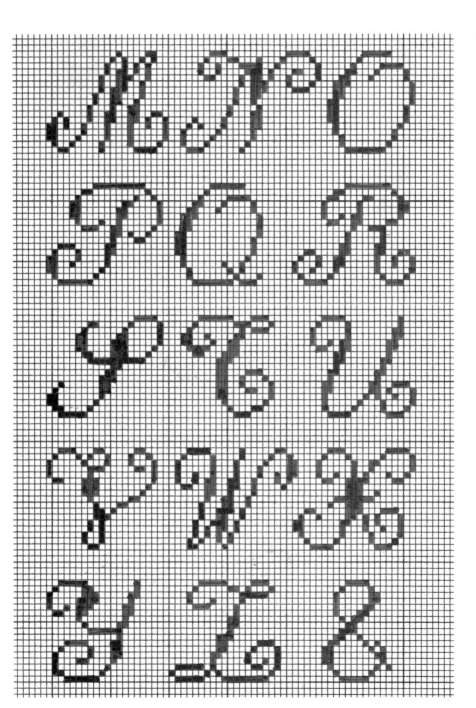

Acknowledgements

A considerable number of people have helped me with this book; some with the stitching of each of the projects. All of them have supported me with tender loving care, a very special thing.

In particular I would like to thank Joan Downes, who, having helped stitch the front cover once, completely restitched it when the format of the book grew a little larger. Others who also stitched my designs were Connie and Ruth Levy, Sally Barratt and Sara Turnbull.

Thanks are also due to Anne Marie Ehrlich and my husband, Patrick, both of whom have been so patient.

Helpful stockists

Dunlincraft
Pullman Road
Wigston
Leicester LE8 2DY
(Importers of DMC stranded cotton)

Appleton Bros Ltd
Church Street
London W4 2PE
(Crewel wool)

Campden Needlecraft Centre
High Street
Chipping Campden
Glos.
(Perforated paper, plastic canvas)

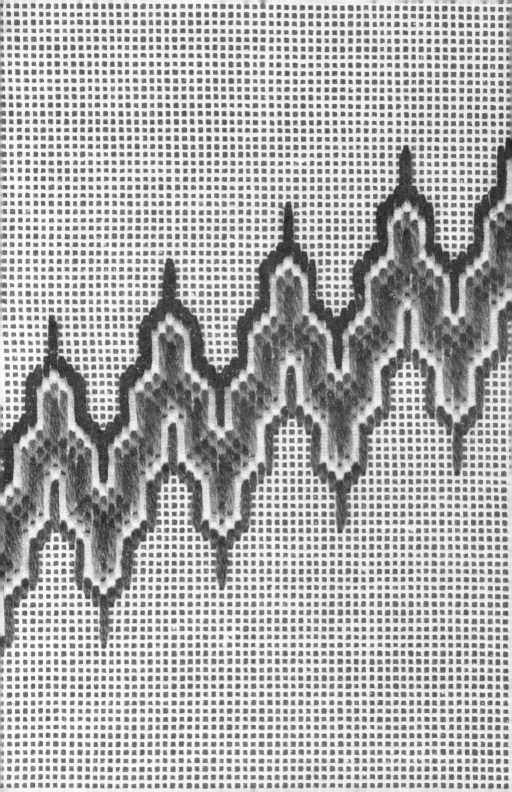